The Duke of Silver River

A Tale of Noahsark

Jo Estell

ISBN 978-1-0980-7122-6 (paperback)
ISBN 978-1-0980-7123-3 (digital)

Christian Faith Publishing, Inc.
832 Park Avenue
Meadville, PA 16335
www.christianfaithpublishing.com

Printed in the United States of America

In a distant castle, in a faraway land, on another world, a woman sat in a large stuffed chair in front of a roaring fireplace surrounded by her family on a cold winter day.

"Grandmother, please tell us a story," piped up the youngest grandchild.

Peering at the boy, a smile tugged at her lips, "A story? Am I now a minstrel to entertain you?"

Another of her grandsons spoke. "Oh, Grandmother, you always tell the most fantastic of tales. Won't you please give forth a story worthy of the Muses?" At his exuberant request, the adults in the room laughed heartily.

Shaking her head, the grandmother said, "With such persuasion and praise, how can I refuse such a simple request?" her eyes twinkled with merriment. "So then, what sort of tale shall I tell?"

The voices of the children rang out their requests, "An adventure."

"A battle."

"A history."

"A tragedy."

"Oh, Grandmother," sighed the oldest girl, "could you possibly tell a love story?"

Her siblings and cousins snickered at her request as their grandmother leaned toward them where they lay sprawled on the floor in front of her and replied, "Well, now, I believe that I can give you a tale with all of those elements."

The children's eyes grew wide with delight as they settled quietly into their cushions, ready for the fabulously wonderful story their grandmother was going to tell.

The father of half of the brood nudged the other with his elbow. "This should be very good, brother, for Mother is truly a weaver of tales."

The other man nodded his agreement. "'Tis the truth, although I think at times it drives Father mad."

Clearing her throat and looking to her sons, the woman said, "If you two are quite finished prattling, I do believe I can begin."

Bowing to her, the men said in unison, "Our apologies, Mother." They sat upon the couch next to their wives and were silent as she tucked her quilt snuggly about her lap and began her story.

"Some time ago, and not so far away, there lived a duke…"

Part 1

After many days of dreary rain, the sun had finally shown its face. A young woman walked briskly down the road to the village. As she arrived, the marketplace was bustling with activity since the village was located on the main road to the royal city. Hawkers cried their wares and services, bargaining and bartering echoed up and down the rows of stalls offering vegetables and meats, clothing, jewelry, weapons, cookware, and numerous other items that a person could want or need. The animals barked, bawled, and squawked from their pens. It was a cacophony of sounds, sights, and smells, and the young woman reveled in it as she browsed among the stalls.

A group of horsemen rode down the center of the street and all moved to the side because it was the vanguard of the royal duke. The woman watched in admiration as the beautiful horses went by, but as a rider rushed to the front of the group, his great horse splashed through a puddle and drenched the young woman in muddy water. The gathered crowd laughed at her sodden plight and she grew angry.

"How now, you fool, look what you have done to me in your haste," she shouted to the rider.

The crowd went silent, for the rider was none other than the duke. He reined his horse around, "You call me a fool, yet I was not the one standing near a puddle."

"Aye, but you were not in the street but upon the sides where the people walk, you should have been more careful."

"The street and walks belong to me—"

"I think not." The crowd gasped at the young woman's audacity.

"What mean you?" the duke demanded

She tilted her head up to look him straight in the eye. "The good people of this town pay you hard-earned rent and taxes for this street, so therefore, I say it belongs to them."

At her words, the duke dismounted and sought to intimidate her, for he was a muscular man and stood a full foot taller than she. But she had no fear of him and stood straight as he put his hands upon her arms as if to throttle her. "Know you not who I am?"

"I know that you are the duke, yet I care not be ye peasant nor prince, for 'twas rude to have your steed stomp in that muddy puddle."

He stepped back from her heated words and flashing eyes, reached into his tunic, pulled out a small bag of coin, and tossed it to her. "Take this then and buy another dress or two if that will soothe thy temper."

Catching the purse, she weighed it carefully, for it was full and could easily support her family for months to come if she chose to keep it. She certainly wouldn't spend it on dresses as the duke had suggested. Instead, she threw it back at his feet, where it landed on the muddy ground, sending another gasp through the crowd.

"I do not want your money; an apology would have sufficed for me. I'll leave you now, for I must wash the mud from this dress, as it is a good one and I wish it not to stain." She turned to walk away as he stooped to pick up the now soiled purse.

"Nay, stay your feet, do not go." He touched her shoulder before she could take a step. "It was crass of me to throw the coin at you. I apologize for your muddying and beseech you to take it. I was in haste for I've just been married and wish to get my bride home."

"Your apology is accepted, milord, but I wish not the coin." She turned to face him, pushing the offered money in his hand away. "Give it to your bride if you must give it away. But I give you fair warning, sir, that she loves another and will die of heartbreak within a year's time."

"You have a harsh tongue on you, wench. Your father would be angry with you for the poor treatment of your betters." The duke put away his purse and mounted his horse.

"My father is wroth with me most times anyhow. But what makes you better than me? Perhaps your wealth and station, but if your flesh is cut, will you not bleed as red as I?"

"What is your name and where is your father, girl? I will speak to him of your insolence."

"I am named Autumn, and Father is at home; our farm is but a mile up the road at the crossroads. He is tending to some repairs upon our house and as such should be quite able to speak with you." She turned and walked away, her head held high.

Autumn made her way slowly to the river, her thoughts lost in her encounter with the duke. She had never seen him up close until today, and he was a handsome devil for sure. She remembered how hard her heart had pounded when he'd dismounted from his horse and towered over her; he was the tallest man she had ever seen. His reddish brown hair was shaggy and fell nearly to his shoulders; he had gray-blue eyes that were set softly into his clean-shaven aristocratic face. Enhanced by the tight woolen jerkin his wide shoulders had tapered to a muscular chest and belly, and the muscles of his legs strained at the seams of his leather breeches, which fit him snugly as they disappeared into boots that laced up to his knees. His hands had been gentle upon her arms even though she knew he wanted to shake her for her bold words, though for a moment she had wished heartily that he would envelope her in his strong embrace.

Autumn was startled at that thought and was immediately ashamed. He was married, hadn't he admitted that? The whole village knew, and Autumn's heart went out to her friend Lucy, who was now the Duchess of Silver River. Lucy was in love with the miller's son, much to the disappointment of her father, a very wealthy merchant who wished his daughter to marry for station rather than love. When word reached him that the duke had been commanded to marry by the king, poor Lucy had no choice but to abide by her father's wishes. Autumn was sure that if Lucy hadn't been so well guarded by her father's men that she and Joshua would have run off together.

Shrugging out of her soiled dress, she put aside all thoughts of the duke and Lucy and focused her attention on cleaning the rapidly drying mud off her good dress. To her dismay, she realized that the mud had soaked completely through to her undergarments and she would have to bathe in the icy water of the river to remove the mud completely from her person. Her younger sister appeared at her side several minutes later. "I've brought your riding clothes, sister. Father is very angry with you. I think you might want to go straight to the training yard instead of the house when you get home. He's mad enough to flog you. The duke, as well as half of the village, has come by to tell him of how you spoke to His Grace. Father says that the duke could have arrested you for speaking to him so in public."

"Then let him do so," grumbled Autumn, stripping to the skin and stepping neck-deep into the river to wash the mud off. "He has ruined my best dress."

"The townspeople say that he gave you a bag of coin and that you threw it back at him. Is that true, sister?"

"Yes, Charilee, it's true."

"Father said that if the duke wasn't already married he would have given you to him. As it is, he's threatened to give you to Michael, who has asked for you many times." Charilee shuddered, for the tanner was an old man, had no teeth, and smelled much like the hides he tanned for a living.

Autumn's eyes flashed. "He wouldn't dare. I'll run off if he tries."

Her sister sighed. "You are foolish to hold out for love. Look at poor Lucy, she's miserable because her father forced her to marry for station, and we all know how much she loves Joshua."

"I could easily love the duke if I allowed myself to," mused Autumn as she dunked her muddy hair into the cold water, "but never the tanner. I feel like retching just at the thought of him, much less in the marriage bed."

"Autumn, such talk is unseemly, even for you," scolded her sister.

"It's true enough. I think that His Grace is an honorable man," she said as she dried off with the towel Charilee provided and changed into her riding clothes while her sister hung the clean dress and undergarments on a bush to dry.

After speaking with Autumn's father, the duke instructed his men to take his wife to the castle. He needed time to think and rode to his favorite spot at the river. He dismounted and tied his horse near the riverbank as he found a tree and sat beneath it. He pondered his situation. His new wife was a weepy thing and very timid. He could not abide such a temperament and wondered what had possessed him to choose her from the many hopefuls that had been at his cousin's court. She was very young, and he was nearly twice her age, but the king had ordered him to marry, and she seemed the least dangerous of his choices. Which brought to mind the she-devil he'd run into in the village. He hadn't meant to drench her in muddy water, and would have apologized, but then she'd yelled at him and called him a fool. At first, he didn't think she realized who he was, until she confessed the opposite, and then he tried to intimidate her, with no success. She looked him square in the eye and told him off. Most women would have wept and moaned about the soaking. Not her; she had gotten angry. He admired her spirit and the way she told him that they were equals because their blood was the same color. His steed, his height, nor his demeanor had intimidated her, and she seemed not to care about his station. He wondered if she ever cried. Somehow he couldn't see her weeping over something trivial like most women. He remembered her dark brown eyes as they threw annoyed sparks of gold at him and how she had struggled with herself over the coin he'd tossed her; somehow he knew that had she kept it she would not have bought dresses.

Suddenly, he heard the voices of two women and the furious splashing of water.

"He has ruined my best dress," growled the voice of the woman who had scolded him in front of the entire village.

Smiling he leaned against the tree trunk and listened to the banter between the two women. He was nearly asleep when a statement perked up his ears.

"I could easily love the duke if I allowed myself to."

A moment later, "I think that His Grace is an honorable man."

He smiled then frowned. Was that wistfulness in her voice? Oh, why did fate have to be so cruel? He bumped his head lightly against the tree trunk several times in frustration. She could very well be his match. He supposed he could take her as his mistress, but the idea did not sit well with him, and he knew that Autumn would spit on him for even suggesting it. Sighing, he went to his horse, mounted, and headed home to his timid bride and a cold dark castle.

Lucy did not die that first year as Autumn had predicted, but she did rub the duke's nerves raw with her constant weeping and wailing. Therefore, he spent most of his time away from his castle, either hunting or at court with his cousin in the City of the Rose.

One day at court, several months into the second year of his marriage to Lucy, the king clapped him on the shoulder. "How is your wife, cousin? I was sure to hear that she was with child by now."

"Nay, milord, I've not been able to get near her with all the fuss she makes. 'Twas a miracle to have gotten through the wedding night."

"Edward, the purpose of the marriage was to conceive an heir."

"Yes, I know, but I should have chosen less hastily."

The king laughed at Edward's crestfallen face. "How, now, cousin, surely it isn't that bad?"

The duke shook his head. "If I come into her chambers, she shrieks as if I am to rape her. A mouse has more courage with a cat."

This brought a bellow of mirth from the king. "Perhaps that spitfire who defied you in the village would have suited you better. Mayhap you should take her as a mistress."

"Cousin, I have thought the same, but she would spit on me and marry the tanner, whom she abhors, before becoming my mistress. Is there no way to annul this fiasco?"

Smiling sadly at the duke, he said, "I'm sorry, Edward, but the marriage cannot be undone. Perhaps the fates will intervene and the gods smile kindly upon you."

"One can only hope, Robert. I suppose I should be going home."

It was a sad ride home for the duke; he was sorely vexed by his unhappy situation. He needed an heir, and his wife was afraid and unwilling. He was not a man of violence and would not force himself upon her. He was also a rare man of fidelity and would not desecrate his vows. Although the thought had occurred to him, he knew that the woman he wanted would refuse him.

The scent of smoke and shouts from his castle brought him out of his gloomy thoughts and he urged his steed into a gallop. When he came through the gates, he could see his bathhouse engulfed in flames. His staff could only keep the fire from spreading to the rest of the castle as the building burned.

Reining his horse close to a stable boy, he shouted to be heard over the roar of the inferno, "What has happened here?"

"No one knows for sure, milord. Milady began to act strange when she received a message from her father earlier today. It is thought that perhaps she has set the place afire in a desperate need to end her life."

Edward dismounted and watched in horror as the structure disappeared in a blaze of red and gold.

Several days later, as the duke sat mounted on his horse watching his servants clean up the debris from the fire, he was confused as to the decision that Lucy had made to suicide. Her charred body had been found in the ruins and placed in the funeral pyre to complete the cremation. Because she had taken her own life, there was no ceremony, and only Edward scattered Lucy's ashes on the banks of Silver River. Autumn had arrived and stood on the opposite side and watched as the deed was done. She had acknowledged him with a nod and left soon after.

A thought came to him and he turned his horse away from the scorched wood, stone, and earth. He kept his horse at a trot as he made his way to Autumn's house. When he arrived, he left his horse's reins to dangle and pounded upon the farmhouse door. A portly man answered and bowed immediately upon seeing the duke.

"Your Grace, 'tis an honor to receive you, milord."

Edward scowled for he disliked the fuss made over his title. "I wish to speak with Autumn."

The farmer's eyes narrowed in anger. "What has that fool girl done this time?"

The duke looked down sternly at the man and was pleased to see him squirm; sometimes his rank had use.

"Apologies, milord, Autumn is in the fields with the yearling horses."

"Thank you." Edward mounted and nudged his steed in the direction indicated by Autumn's father.

The sight he encountered took his breath away as he saw the woman he was seeking riding a young horse bareback across the field. Her long brown hair was bound in a thick plait that trailed down her back, but as the colt galloped through the grass, it flew out behind her like a golden banner. Her face was alight with the pure joy of riding the animal. Suddenly the colt spooked and reared. Edward held his breath as Autumn held tight to the horse. He thought for sure that she would fall, but she stayed put, and before he could move to assist her, the colt came down. Instead of calming, however, he bucked, and the duke feared again for her safety. He expected her to be thrown over the horse's head. He sat mesmerized as the young woman expertly brought the animal under control, laughing the whole time.

"She's a fair hand at breaking them in, Your Grace. 'Tis a bit of a shock to you, milord?"

The duke turned his eyes down to the speaker, still a bit dazed at the sight he had witnessed. It was Autumn's mother.

"I thought for certain she'd be thrown," he said as he dismounted.

"She's a way with the creatures. Broke the very steed you ride, milord."

Looking to the very large horse beside him, he said, "Indeed?"

"Aye, milord, though he'd not yet reached his full growth. She loved this one, sire, even named him, but her father had already sold him to you."

Edward's curiosity was piqued. "Named him what?"

"Prince; she said that he had a regal bearing about him."

At her statement, his horse snorted and tossed its head. Edward laughed and patted the flank fondly. "He does indeed. I wish to speak with your daughter, if I may interrupt her labors."

"I'll fetch her immediately, milord."

As the duke watched Autumn's mother head toward the corral, he thought of the young woman he'd just seen riding the wild horse. She had a free spirit, and her parents could see that forcing her to conform to traditional standards would stifle and depress her, so they allowed her to pursue her interests. Although, Edward thought, a tighter rein on her tongue wouldn't hurt.

He had often found an excuse to go into the village to try to get a glimpse of her. He'd not spoken with her since the day she'd yelled at him, but he often saw her walking on the road or through the marketplace, and though he knew they weren't for him, the sight of her smiles soothed him. He had watched from a distance as she spoke to everyone who crossed her path; she always had a grin at the ready. He remembered one day when he'd gone to the blacksmith, for Prince had thrown a shoe. He usually tried to stay inconspicuous, but Troy, an irritating old man who plagued everyone with his incessant complaints about nearly everything, had spotted him and headed in his direction. Edward had rolled his eyes and sighed, and by chance had made eye contact with a smiling Autumn; the resulting jolt had stunned him. He then observed as she cleverly maneuvered the man away from him. He still wondered what she had told Troy to send him on his way.

Hoof beats brought the duke back to the present and he watched as Autumn cantered toward him on a new mount. He noticed that she wore a loose tunic and breeches instead of a dress.

"You wish to speak with me, Your Grace?"

"Aye, will you ride with me?"

"As you wish, milord."

He mounted and turned Prince to the road as she moved her horse beside him. He could see the confusion and puzzlement on her face.

"Milord," she paused to gather her thoughts, "I'm sorry for your loss, sire. Lucy was a close friend, and I will grieve, but what need hast thou of me?"

He smiled internally at her formal way of speaking. He also heard the sorrow in her voice and said, "I know that this is improper..."

At that, she snorted much like Prince had earlier. "Nonsense, you are the duke. Let old Troy moan about it and the others wonder, but who are they to tell you what to do and how to act?"

Edward blinked at the ferocity in her statement and smiled sadly. "I've asked for you, because you are well liked and respected in town. As such I am wondering if you may have an answer for me."

She stiffened on her horse's back, bare, he noticed, of any saddle. "I am not a gossipmonger, but if I can aid thee, I will try."

Slowing his horse to a walk, he looked to her and asked plaintively, "Why would she take her own life? Do they think that I was cruel to her?"

He could see by her expression that she was taken aback by the questions, and he respected that she took her time in answering. "Sometimes, a few of your house servants would mention how Lucy would wail when you visited her chambers, but I stopped that talk when I could. I know that you are not a cruel person and you were not mean to her. Lucy was very timid; she would bow in the wind like a willow. She loved Joshua, the miller's son, and he loved her, and I think that she thought that by keeping you from her bed, the king would have no choice but to dissolve the marriage."

"How do you know that I'm not a cruel man?" Edward was curious to hear her answer.

"Your steed, milord; a cruel man would treat his animals as harshly as his people. Your mount is in pristine form; therefore, logic dictates that you are not a cruel man."

The duke stopped his horse and smiled at her. "Have you met many cruel men?"

Her answer shocked him. "Just one. He is from the Realm, and it is said that he has banished his own daughter to the dreaded forest of Darkwater. When I saw him, his horse's flanks were bloody and a loose shoe had torn its hoof, yet he refused to let the creature rest."

Edward knew of the man. "He is Molsen, a vile man indeed." He changed the subject. "But why would Lucy take her own life?"

"Because Joshua knew that after all this time, the king would not annul your marriage and did his duty to his family by marrying Sophie, one of Lucy's cousins. She lost hope then, sire, and that is why she took her life. Her light was gone and she had no courage to make it work with you. She was very narrow-minded when it came to loving Joshua."

He sat quietly for several long moments digesting what Autumn had said. "Will you come to the castle tomorrow and take care of the removal of her things? Her father doesn't want them, and I'm not sure what to do."

"Surely, you have servants who can fulfill that task, milord."

"Aye, servants I have, but they do not have your knowledge of Lucy, nor do they possess your compassion."

"Then I shall be honored to do as you have requested. I really must get back to my chores, sire."

"On the morrow then?"

"On the morrow," Autumn agreed as she turned her horse toward home and kicked the filly into a gallop.

Edward watched until she vanished over a hill and then nudged Prince into a canter. Somehow, he felt bereft without her near.

She could not believe her good fortune. The duke had asked a special favor of her. Perhaps, if she pleased him at this task she could one day work in his household. She pushed the other thought away. She was not suited to marry the king's cousin, being a poor farmer's daughter, and did not even allow herself to entertain the idea; although, she had felt breathless when he turned those beautiful gray-blue eyes on her. She finished her chores and checked on the horses before supper, but she was anxious to be finished with the meal and abed.

"Sister, are you ill? Your face is flushed and you have fidgeted all through supper."

"Nay, Charilee, I'm not ill, just a bit tired as the horses were a bit fractious today."

"What did the duke wish of you, daughter?" her father asked.

"He beseeched me to help remove Lucy's things. He wishes me to go tomorrow."

"Has he no servants?"

"He has servants, Father, but they are still busy cleaning up the debris from the fire, and he confided in me that I would be more discreet than they."

"Well, then, off to bed with you," her mother said.

"But the dishes, Mother, it is my turn tonight."

"Nonsense, Autumn, you've had a busy day and you are sure to have a trying one tomorrow, for I know your heart daughter. 'Twill be a sad thing for you to do as I know though her family is wealthy and we are not, you were a friend to that dear soul."

"I love you, Mama, thank you." Autumn kissed her mother's cheek then placed one on her father's balding head. "You too, Papa."

"Good night, daughter," he said as she left.

Upon entering her room, she washed with tepid water from a basin and changed into her nightgown. She unbound her hair and brushed it thoroughly before braiding it again. She crawled into bed and was asleep almost before her head hit the pillow.

Autumn woke before the rooster's crow the next morning and dressed quickly in her riding clothes. She rode the spirited colt she had broken the day before and reveled in his gallop. As she approached the castle, she slowed her mount and had him walk slowly up the cobbled path to the broad courtyard. As she entered the walls, she could see the large square of scorched earth where the bathhouse had stood and felt sad, but she marveled at the architecture of the castle. It was ancient but sturdy and well cared for; the walls were high, smooth, and slanted slightly at an outward angle negating the need for a moat. Three tall towers rose from the center of the building and she wondered at the rooms situated there.

The sound of men shouting and a horse's scream caught her attention, so she nudged her colt into a trot. She saw red at the sight that greeted her. A large stallion was rearing and neighing as a stableman snapped a whip over his head in an effort to control him. Autumn inserted herself between the men and the angry horse, shouting, "You are fools to treat him so." She grasped the stallion's bridle and, in a move that stopped all activity in the courtyard, swung from the colt's back to his.

"You fool girl, he's not been broke," the horse master yelled.

She yelled right back, "You are the fool; the whip was driving him mad. You must treat such creatures with respect."

Autumn stroked the neck of the great beast knowing that he'd try to throw her soon. She could feel the tremors in his muscles as they bunched for bucking. Leaning forward and whispering in the large ear, she said, "Come now, big fella, I'll not hurt you. I've gotten them to stop the whip; surely you can be kind to me." Settling into position, she shouted to the others, "Back away, he'll be kicking in a moment."

She was very nervous. He was a big horse, and the ground was cobblestones, not the soft sweet grass of her training pasture, but she shook off her fear and waited. She didn't wait long before his head went down and his tail came up. He then reared to have the unfamiliar weight off his back. Holding tight to his mane, she brought him down only to have him buck again. He spiraled around the small enclosure, bucking frantically, but the young woman remained calmly seated on her unwilling mount. Eventually he stopped his tantrum and allowed Autumn to guide him to the stable and into a stall. As she slid off the great back, the men looked at her in amazement.

"I've never seen the like," muttered one as she closed the stall door and patted the stallion's nose.

Stepping out of the stable, she went to her colt that was being held by one of the stable boys.

"Your saddle is absent, miss," he noted.

"I rarely use it. Please see to my horse and make sure he is secure. He has a tendency to spook."

"Yes, miss."

"Thank you," Autumn called after the boy as he led the colt into the stable.

A woman rushed to her and gave a half curtsy. "His Grace is expecting you, miss. Please follow me."

Smiling at the woman, Autumn nodded and followed her into the castle.

Edward had seen Autumn swing onto the stallion and his heart leapt into his throat as he watched the brute try to throw her. He was incredulous that she'd been able to calm him, and then he remembered that her mother had said she had a gift with the animals. The duke's gaze followed her as his servant led her into his home, then he turned from the window and met them at the head of the stairs.

The young woman gave a deep curtsy and said, "Milord, I am here as you have requested."

A smile twitched at his lips as he dismissed the servant. "'I am glad that you have come."

He ushered her to the rooms that had once been occupied by Lucy. He saw Autumn's eyes widen at the sight of the large chamber. It was filled with a massive canopy bed, heavy pink velvet curtains tied at the posts. Several wardrobes and armoires were lined up against the walls, and a vanity with a large glass mirror sat next to the bed. Edward showed her to the closets adjoining the room; they were filled to bursting with silks and satins.

"This was all Lucy's. I have no idea what to do with it, and her father does not want it, so whatever ideas you may have, I'm listening. Perhaps you know someone who could use all of this?"

"Your Grace, I only know the people of the village, and the women there have no use for silks and satins. They work hard, and stout woolen dresses do not fray easily."

"Perchance they could be used for a celebration?"

"Aye, but these are suited for a palace, milord, not a country tavern. Besides, times have been quite harsh lately and no one has time or coin for a party."

Edward was stunned by Autumn's revelations and respected her candor, but her next statement surprised him further. "Sophie may like to have a few, as would my sister Charilee."

"Choose some for yourself as well."

"Nay, sire, that I cannot do, for my friend was much smaller than I and they will not fit."

Edward stepped close to her and put his hands to her shoulders, and as her brown eyes met his, he had an incredible urge to kiss her. He gave into it and the shock that went through him nearly sent him to his knees. Autumn was a willing participant at first, but when she realized what was happening, she stepped quickly away as if burned.

"Milord, 'tis not appropriate."

"For a man to kiss a beautiful woman?"

Autumn flushed with the praise and responded, "Nay, the timing, sire. Lucy is but a fortnight beyond this world, and though I know you held little love for her, she should still be honored for at least a month of mourning."

Impressed by her loyalty, he conceded. "After the month has ended, will you become my wife?"

She turned her brown eyes to him wide with confusion, and for a moment, he thought that she would swoon. Instead she blinked and said to him, "Milord, I am but a poor farmer's daughter and have no dowry to bring to thee. Besides, I have a sharp tongue and would be apt to offend many at court—"

Edward enveloped her in his arms his tunic deftly muffling her protests. "I care neither for coin nor dowry, and thy sharp tongue can be trained, though I do like a good row now and again. Fear not that your station is too low, because my heart has fallen for you."

"Play not with me, be ye royal duke or nay," she said, pushing out of his embrace. "I'm no timid mouse as thy late wife, but I wish not the pain of trickery."

He fell to his knees and spread his arms wide. "I swear to thee that this is no trickery. I'd even told my cousin that I wished I had met you before my marriage to Lucy, for I'd have chosen you instead."

Edward saw her swallow hard, still looking at him suspiciously. Her eyes narrowed then widened. "Pray, tell me that you're not speaking of the king?"

When he nodded affirmative, she put her face in her hands and wailed in despair, "Oh, he must think me a shrew."

The duke stood, grasped her hands, and looked into her eyes. "My dear lady, he actually said that you would suit me well."

She tugged to be released, but Edward pulled her close instead. "My life had been stagnant until the day I muddied your dress. I still think often of that day. Most girls would have wept and wailed, but you shouted at me and called me a fool. I tried to intimidate you, yet you had no fear of me. Another would have taken that bag of coin, but you threw it back at me. I need a woman with your spirit and strength. I think I fell in love with you on that day so long ago. Please, say that you'll be my wife."

Stepping back from him, she put her hands to the sides of his face and drew his head down to hers. Looking square into his blue-gray eyes, she said, "After the month of mourning, I will marry you, but in a simple ceremony here without all the pomp and nonsense." She kissed him hard on the mouth, and before he could react, she had slipped from his embrace and made her way to one of the closets.

Edward sat and watched her sort through the clothing for a while before becoming restless and moving to her side. "Can I help?" he asked.

"Give me an idea as to whom to give all these dresses to. There must surely be one here for every day of the year. Why would a person need so many? I only have my riding clothes and five woolen dresses. I need no more than that."

He sat on a bench near the closet that Autumn was perusing, a grin on his face. "These are just the day dresses."

Autumn looked at him sharply. "What?!"

Laughing at the incredulous tone in her voice, he pointed to a set of large wardrobes across the room. "Those hold the evening dresses and ball gowns."

Sitting next to Edward on the bench, she huffed, "What is the purpose of changing your gown halfway through the day? Such a waste of time." A thought occurred to her. "I'll not be changing every hour when I'm your wife, that's plain foolish."

Pulling her into a hug, he whispered in her ear, "I'd prefer you wear nothing at all."

She moved away as if stung. "Your Grace, what a shameful thing to say."

Drawing her back, he said, "Call me Edward. I can't stand all the milords and Your Graces I get on a daily basis."

"It would not be proper for me to call you by your given name, milord."

The duke rolled his eyes and grinned mischievously at Autumn. "'Tis not proper to yell at the royal duke and call him a fool either."

She gave him a sour look.

"Besides," he said softly, "I wish to hear you speak my name."

"But…"

"Please?"

"Thou art a stubborn man, milord Edward."

The day grew late and still Autumn sorted through the clothes that had belonged to Lucy. They had been good friends, but she was disgusted by the amount of clothing the deceased woman had accumulated.

"I know not why she'd need all of this," she muttered to herself as she dug into an armoire filled to bursting with undergarments. Her hand bumped something hard at the very back; she pulled out a large wooden box and opened it. On the very top was a letter addressed to her in Lucy's handwriting. Breaking the seal with an unsteady hand, she read the letter and her eyes filled with tears, for in the written words she could feel Lucy's pain.

My Dearest Autumn,

Many a day I have envied you for your freedom and your boldness. I am not a courageous girl to defy my father as you have done with yours so often, for it is Joshua whom I love. I told Papa so, but he would have none of it, saying that he has not worked so hard so that I would marry a poor miller's son. He wanted me to marry well, but even in his dreams, he did not aspire to the royal family. How I begged and cried to him, but he grew angry then, and Papa can be mean when he is angry, so I stopped my pleading. I did not want to hurt my beloved, but Father had no interest in granting me happiness, and when he heard that the duke was ordered to marry, I was sponsored immediately. I'll never know why milord chose me, but I was devastated, as Papa had wanted me to raise my station and you can't get much higher than a duchess. I wished to petition the king, but alas, I was a coward. 'Twas my duty to do my father's will, and so it was done. The day milord drenched you with muddy water was the last day of my life, yet when I heard you yell, I peeked through the windows of the carriage. I feared for you when he dismounted, but you stood fast and feared him not, and, oh, to toss his coin back at his feet and refuse his misguided charity. I thought

23

for sure you'd be arrested, but then I saw the look in his eyes and knew that his heart was gone to you, although I'm sure that neither of you could see it, angry as you both were. I prayed to the fates and the gods, begging that the king would annul my marriage, yet they did not listen. And when Joshua did his duty and married my cousin Sophie, my heart shattered as a crystal upon the cobblestones. I knew it was my time to leave this world. I have obtained a vial of opiates and will drink it tonight when I go for my evening bath. I will sit in the tub in my favorite dress, so as not to embarrass the poor soul who finds me. I am afraid of life without Joshua and cannot continue knowing that he has found another to replace me so quickly. His Grace is a kind and gentle man, but I cannot give him the life he deserves, for I am not the woman that he wants.

I know how you love to read, so I have left you your favorites from my library in this box. I have also left a locket that your sister fancied. Please give it to her and thank her for being my friend. And though Charilee was my best friend, you knew me best, and I have no doubt that His Grace will ask you to clear my chambers.

I beg of thee forgiveness.

Your loving friend,
Lucy

Such is how Edward found her, with the cherished books in her lap and tears silently streaming down her face, surrounded by piles of underwear.

He rushed to her side, for he had never seen her in tears. "My dearest, what troubles thee?"

She lifted her sad brown eyes to his and handed him Lucy's letter.

"You've read this?"

"Aye, milord, Lucy's tutor taught me when we were children; I was quite fond of her library."

They sat in silence as the duke read Lucy's letter. "You were right about Joshua, and it seems as if the fire was an accident."

Autumn only nodded. Edward knelt in front of her, pushing aside a pile of bloomers. He took a silk handkerchief from his doublet pocket and gently dried her face.

"Come," he said quietly, "I've ordered supper prepared."

"Supper!" She stood so quickly that she nearly cracked her head on his chin. "I best be getting home, sire."

The duke stood and grasped her arm gently. "Nay, I've sent word that you are staying the night."

Wide-eyed and angry she growled, "'Twill cause a scandal. You should've asked me first. Now what am I to do? Father will be wroth with me again and I did naught wrong this time."

Edward tugged at her and brought her close; he bent his head and placed a kiss on her forehead. He could see worry and anger in her eyes as he said, "The king has summoned me, so I must leave tonight. There will be no scandal, but the village is abuzz about your time spent here today."

She leaned her forehead on his muscular chest and muttered, "I'll box their ears if I hear a word of it."

The duke laughed. "That's my girl. Come, let us eat so that I may be on my way. I've had your room prepared and fresh clothing brought. Fear not, my love, that I'll take advantage."

Straightening, she thumped his chest with her fist. "As if I'd allow such a thing."

He chuckled as he took her hand and led her out of Lucy's room. "I've something I want to show you before we eat."

Curious, she let him lead her out of the gloomy chamber and followed him quietly as he led her up the spiral stairs to the top of the middle tower. He stopped in front of a set of tall, wide doors that had been intricately carved with his crest, a white winged horse rearing on a forest green background of oak trees with a silver river flowing through the center. He pushed them open and Autumn was breathless with awe. The room sprawled the entire length and width of the tower and was at least three stories in height. Tall narrow windows filled with precious glass let in the fading glow of the evening sun. But what left her speechless were the thousands of books that lined the shelves from floor to ceiling.

Before she could take a step forward, Edward blocked her way and shut the doors. "First, my love, we eat, then I promise that you can visit this room anytime and as often as you wish."

He grinned at her disappointment, kissed the tip of her nose, and puffed out his chest. "What reward do I get from thee, milady, for having shown you my room of wonders?"

Autumn's eyes misted at his kindness and she sighed. "My dearest Edward, a lifetime of gratitude and love for such a precious gift." She grasped him in a tight hug. "Thank you, milord."

He took her hand in his again, "Come then, supper is waiting."

As they traversed the stairs down the tower and made their way to the dining room, Autumn remembered that Edward had said he'd been summoned by the king. When they were seated and the meal served, she asked, "Is there trouble, sire, that your cousin calls for you?"

Edward shook his head. "Nay, Robert often calls for me when the mood suits him. Methinks he'll order me to marry again."

"Surely, he'll allow a time of mourning for poor Lucy." Autumn was indignant at a perceived insult to her late friend.

"I plan on telling him that we'll be married in a month's time in a simple ceremony here."

She smiled at him then sobered as a thought came to her. "What if he says no?"

The duke set down his fork. "I've already told you that he said you'd suit me well, and would it be so bad to wed sooner?"

"'Twill be as His Majesty wishes," Autumn said quietly.

Edward resumed his meal as the young woman picked at the last of her food.

"Edward?" she spoke softly.

He looked up and smiled at her, pleased that she had used his name. "Yes?"

"If the king insists on getting us wed now, will you beseech him to allow us to have the ceremony here instead of at the Rose Palace? I know Lucy in her own way gave us her blessing, but many in the village would like to be a part of it and cannot travel so far."

With supper finished and the dishes cleared, the duke rose from his chair and stood next to her, as he bent to her ear he whispered, "Worry not, love, I'm sure that he'll agree. Robert is a very reasonable man."

He pulled out her chair, tugged her to her feet, then waved over a maid and said, "Muriel will show you to your room. I promise to be back as soon as I am able."

Autumn hugged him fiercely. "Do be careful, milord, for the way shall soon be dark."

He returned the hug and set her away from him as he bowed with a flourish. "It shall be as my lady commands."

She laughed and swatted at him. "Away with you, you fool. I shall see you tomorrow eve."

Edward hurried to the stable after Autumn had followed the maid out of the room. He was pleased to see that his horse was ready and mounted up. He kicked Prince into a gallop, and as he thought about Autumn's request to have the wedding at his castle rather than the king's, he wondered what his cousin's response would be. He arrived at the palace an hour later and was curious as to the commotion at the gates.

"Who goes there?" a guard's voice shouted from the ramparts. "State thy name and business."

"I am Lord Edward, Duke of Silver River. I've come at the king's command."

Peering down at the duke, the guard shouted, "Raise the gate, 'tis the king's cousin."

Edward rode through the gate as it rose and headed for the stables. The courtyard was ablaze with torchlight while the royal guard and men at arms dashed hither and thither. Edward left Prince in the capable hands of a stable lad and rushed into the palace. He hurried to the throne room with a sense of dread. The state of chaos in that large chamber took the duke by surprise and saw that his cousin was having difficulty restoring order. He bellowed, "How, now, what is all this commotion?"

Instantly the room quieted and all turned in his direction. A few of the minor nobles bowed to him as he made his way to his cousin's side. He acknowledged them with a nod.

"I say, Edward, have you been taking shouting lessons from your village spitfire?"

Many laughed at the king's jest, easing some of the tension that had filled the room.

"Nay, I've not given her a reason to shout at me lately." Another round of laughter ensued. "What has happened, Robert, for never have I seen the gates closed."

"An assassin has tried to murder my infant son," the king's voice was grave. "Thank the gods that the plot was foiled."

Edward clasped his cousin's shoulder. "Did you catch them?"

The king nodded. "Aye, they are outlaws exiled from the Realm."

"Not from Molsen's daughter's group?"

"Nay, she and her people were devoured by the Dark Forest; no one has seen nor heard from them since she was banished. It has been assumed that they are dead." Robert paced the floor a moment before sitting upon the edge of his throne. "These are vile men of Molsen's ilk, rotten to the core. I once met Tarynn. She was a kind soul, strong willed, and independent, but that is a necessity as Molsen is a violent drunk. I heard that he chained her to a wall and murdered her best friend in front of her."

Edward sat on the throne next to Robert's and asked, "Was Matek injured?" When the king shook his head, the duke continued, "Why kill a newborn child? Makes more sense to go after you."

"I agree, but the prisoners began muttering about some prophecy. I couldn't make sense of it, and I know that you have studied the histories, so perchance you can explain what it means."

"I'll do my best, Majesty, but it might be best to bring them in one at a time. Perhaps we can catch them in a lie."

"A wise strategy, cousin." The king motioned to the guard to bring in the first of the three prisoners. The men of the nobility lined the walls of the throne room as the man was brought in. He was short and bone thin, dressed in rags he looked to be an old man.

Edward stood and stepped off the throne dais. He was generally a laidback, easygoing man, but he did not tolerate threats to his king nor his family. Being a very tall man, the tallest in the kingdom, he had a distinct advantage in intimidation. Not that it worked on Autumn, he thought. In addition to his great height, he was broad of chest and muscular from years on horseback, swordplay, and other games of war. The guard had thrown the prisoner to the floor and he had remained there, whether out of insolence or weakness, no one was sure. As he stood over the crumpled man, Edward nudged him with the tip of his boot. "Get up, I wish to speak with you."

The man gave a choke of insane laughter but did not move.

The duke nudged him harder this time and motioned for two of the guardsman to lift him to his feet. They picked him up by his arms, but the prisoner refused to cooperate, letting his legs remain limp beneath him. Instead, he cackled like a madman and said, "The future king will be allied with the Kingdom of Darkwater and peace shall reign. Darkwater is impregnable, so the son of the present king must die." The prisoner's words brought a shocked silence to the room, and Robert had turned pale.

"Lies!" he shouted.

"Nay, cousin, he speaks the truth. The histories do speak of a prophecy that says the Rose Kingdom will join with Darkwater to combat a great evil, but I do not recall a specific time given."

"The forest is nothing but strange beasts and trees," commented Wester, the Duke of Windy Glen. "Most men never return if they enter it, but the rare few that have come back seem to be somewhat daft and terrified of the place."

The imprisoned man gave another burst of crazy laughter and said, "A warrior within the depths of the Dark Forest is preparing an army to conquer the world. Such has my master told me."

Edward glowered at the man. "And who is thy master?"

A shriek came from the depths of the captive and he writhed as if in great pain. His eyes rolled to the back of his head and he moved no more. As he called for his healer, the king instructed the guard to release the prisoner. They did and let him fall hard to the floor. A guard who had been with the other prisoners followed the healer into the room. "Majesty, the others have died."

"What say you?" demanded Robert.

"They thrashed as if in great pain and then fell dead upon the floor."

"There is an evil magic here, sire. The bodies must be burned immediately," said the healer.

"Then do it."

After the dead fugitive's body was removed, an uneasy silence fell amongst the men.

"Cousin, why hast thou sent for me?" Edward asked quietly.

"I know that your wife is but a fortnight departed, but you must find another to wed soon."

"I've found her, but she wishes a month of mourning for her friend."

"Is she mad? Mourn a suicide?" Robert exclaimed.

"She also requested that should you say no to the period of mourning that we be married in a simple ceremony at Silver River."

The king looked to his cousin. "This is the wench who called you a fool? The one you spoke of refusing to be your mistress?"

"Aye, milord, though I never did ask her to be my mistress. She has spirit and passion, no mouse she; she is not intimidated by me in the least. And she loves me, not for my wealth, but my heart."

"How do you know this, cousin?"

"The day I muddied her, I tossed her a full purse. She threw it back at me saying that she did not want my coin."

"Are there witnesses to this?"

"Nearly the whole village of Silver River."

Robert threw back his head and gave a great shout of laughter. "I shall grant her boon of a ceremony at your castle, but in a week you shall be wed."

"Thy wish is my command." Edward bowed to his king. "May I take your leave? I wish to be home by daybreak."

"Be cautious, cousin, the way is dark, and after tonight, who knows what is waiting for our family," the king said as he embraced the duke and sent him on his way.

Edward was home before the sun broke the horizon. He left Prince in the stable master's care and hurried into the castle. Stopping by the kitchen to grab a bit of bread, he encountered Autumn. She was sitting at the servants' table, a lantern burning brightly and a book in front of her. The duke smiled to himself, leaned against the doorframe, and observed how the lantern light flickered on her face and hair. He was content to watch her forever. Her eyes held a far-away look and he wondered at the tale she was reading. The head cook spied Edward standing there as she came in to prepare for the morning meal.

"Your Grace, we weren't expecting you to be back so soon," she bellowed.

Autumn jumped in fright and then quietly shut her book. "Milord, have you slept at all this night?"

He straightened and stretched, drawing out a yawn. "Nay, milady, I've not, and I've asked you to call me Edward."

Grabbing the book from the table, she took him by the hand. "To bed with thee then."

Feigning reluctance to follow her, he asked, "How knowest you where my chambers are?"

"Because I asked, and lo and behold they are next door to mine."

He laughed and dropped her hand, but grabbed her by the waist and swung her in a circle. He set her on her feet but did not release her. Looking in her eyes, he saw joy but a lingering worry as well. "What troubles thee, my love?" He smoothed her eyebrow with his thumb as he placed a hand to her cheek.

"What did the king say, milord?" Her brown eyes were wide with hope.

"'You are to call me Edward." He placed a kiss upon her forehead. "He commanded that we be wed within the week."

Autumn sighed. "That answer was to be expected, but as to the place, milord?" At the duke's stern look, she rolled her eyes. "Edward."

He pulled her fully into his embrace as he told her, "Robert has granted your request, and we shall be married here."

When they had reached his rooms, she stopped at the doorway. "Come and lay with me tonight," Edward pleaded with her, "for my bed is cold and empty."

Autumn balked at his suggestion. "And so it shall remain until we are wed." So saying, she turned and entered her room, shutting the door firmly behind her. Edward laughed, shut his door, and stripped off his clothes. He climbed beneath the blankets and lay back on the pillows, comparing his late wife to his soon-to-be bride. They were as night was to day, and he knew that once they were wed, Autumn would never deny him her bed. When he held her, he felt the passion flow through her and he knew that his touch affected her as hers affected him. Soon, however, the exertions of the night lulled him and he fell into a deep sleep.

Autumn had not slept either, she had visited the library after being shown to her room and had read through the night. She'd been worried about Edward's journey to the royal city in the dark. Crime rarely occurred, but there were wolves and lions that would attack a lone person on occasion. She had spent much thought on what it meant to be Edward's wife, and as duchess she would have the power to help those in need in the village. She had also found a solution to the removal of Lucy's things. She had found a dress that suited for her wedding gown and thankfully had found another in the exact same material to supplement an alteration. She hadn't been sure what to do with the jewelry, so she had moved the chest to her own room until she decided. The books were moved to the library, and the knickknacks, mementos, and other odds and ends would be given to Joshua. She would have Sophie and Charilee pick out several gowns for their own, and with the remainder, she would set up a shop to sell in the village.

Autumn was taller and broader than most in the town. Because of her penchant for horses, she was actually quite muscular; she was strong both physically and mentally and could handle herself quite well. Her father had said that her physique was a throwback to ancient times when a woman had needed to be fierce and strong; as such, she fit Edward well, for they were both unique in a land of normal. Her last thought before sleep overtook her was that she needed to hire a seamstress to alter her gown.

Raised voices woke Edward several hours later. He rolled out of bed and pulled on his breeches. Opening the door to the hallway, he watched in fascination as Autumn faced down the head housekeeper.

"You call yourself a hardworking servant, yet you seem to laze about and do nothing. This castle is filthy, and the king shall be here at the end of the week. You need to scour every inch of this place, starting now!" Autumn shouted.

Apparently the servant took offense at being told what to do by a mere village girl. "Who are you to be ordering me and my girls about?" the older woman snarled back.

Speaking quietly from his bedroom door, Edward said, "The lady is to be my wife, so whatever she asks of you, you shall obey."

Autumn looked in his direction, and her eyes widened at the sight of his bare chest and tousled hair. A slow smile curved his lips as he realized that it was his lack of a tunic, not his words, that had left her speechless. He gave her a wink. He scowled at the servant. "Did you not hear?"

The older woman snapped to attention, as she too had been stunned at the duke's appearance. "Aye, milord." She gave a deep curtsy. "It shall be done as you command. I will spread the word." To Autumn she said stiffly, "My apologies, milady, all will be done as you have requested."

"I thank you," Autumn replied offhandedly and dismissed the servant, distracted by Edward's state of undress. As the woman left to gather the others to tackle the enormous chore of cleaning the castle in a week's time, Autumn went to Edward and said, "Milord, thou truly art a giant." Shaking her head to clear it, she stiffened her spine. "'Tis indecent to be dressed so…" Her words trailed off as he took her hand and pulled her gently to him; he drew her slowly into his chamber and shut the door softly with his foot. He placed her hands upon his bare chest taking care not to startle her. Though he was nearing forty, he was healthy and looked much younger than his actual years. His arms and chest were finely muscled from years of wrestling and swordplay and the thews of his legs were solid and strong from constant horseback riding. He had won many a tournament in his life because of his very size and strength.

He held Autumn's hands softly to his chest and nudged her chin to look into her eyes. He saw the heat of desire burning deep in the golden brown orbs as well as apprehension. Strong and tall compared to the woman of the village she may be, but still petite compared to his large frame.

"Does my great size worry you, my love?" he phrased the question quietly.

"Nay, Edward, I know the basics of the mating ritual, for my mother thought it best to inform me. What I fear is that I won't be able to please thee."

Kneeling before her, he moved her hands to his shoulders and leaned his head upon her breast. "You please me by not shying from my embrace or my touch. I hear your heart beat strong, and it's the sound of a fearless soul. Truly thou art the mate the gods have meant for me." He wrapped his strong arms around her as she dropped her chin to the top of his head and caressed the back of his neck.

Autumn brushed his shaggy hair with her fingers. "'Tis I who am blessed, for verily I despaired at ever finding love. Never, my dearest Edward, did I dream to find it in such grand scale, for I'd have been happy to wed a stable boy for a simple thing as love."

Looking up at her, he grinned with mischief. "Then a stable boy I shall become."

Laughing, the young woman pushed out of his embrace. "Thou art a fool, you silly man, for I love you as you are."

Edward got to his feet and lunged for her, but she was quick and danced away from his grasp. "Nay, milord, I'll not lay with you until our wedding night."

The duke let out a mock groan as he threw himself backward upon his bed, the frame creaking under his weight. "Thou art cruel to tease me so."

Feigning indignation, Autumn cried out, "I tease thee? I'm not the one wandering the castle half dressed, Edward!"

Sitting up, he gave a laugh. "Well said, milady, well said." Pleading with his eyes, he continued, "Is there no small reward for my imposed distress? A tiny kiss upon my cheek perchance?"

"I trust thee not; you'll have me upon your bed in but a moment should I step near."

Edward put his hands behind his back. "I give you my word that all I wish is but a simple kiss. To drink of your love from your lips must tide me over for the week, for to me it seems a year."

Autumn edged closer to him, still wary of a trick. "I can grant you a kiss, my love. One a day to sate thy heart, for I too wish to be with you and feel the time crawl slowly."

She reached his bed and placed a soft kiss upon his lips. As she pulled away, he whispered, "Do not go yet, my dear, another do I wish from you, for truly do I hunger for your touch."

"Milord, I beg of thee, do not tease, for I must be true to myself, and I desire you something fierce."

"Just one more and I release you to your duties."

She complied, and he placed his hands upon her face, deepening the kiss. He was satisfied to hear her whimper. He released her quickly for his control was fading. "Go, love, and prepare, for on sixth day we shall be wed."

As Autumn scurried out of his chamber, he lay back on his bed and groaned.

Several minutes after the encounter with the duke in his chambers, Autumn set forth to the village to obtain the services of a seamstress. She was quite at home on horseback and repairing saddles and tack. She could even make fine stitches in someone's flesh, but when it came to needle and thread on cloth, Autumn was all thumbs. She set her colt to a sedate pace and lost herself in the thought of her upcoming nuptials. The sound of a galloping horse drew her attention, and as she looked up, Edward raced past.

"Where are you going in such haste?" she shouted.

"To the river!" came his reply.

Autumn laughed as she continued on her way. Arriving at the village several minutes later, she dismounted and led her horse to the dressmaker's shop. As she entered the small establishment, all talk ceased and everyone's eyes were on her. Thinking nothing of the strange behavior, Autumn asked to see the proprietor of the shop. He approached and asked her in a cold voice, "What can I assist you with?"

"I wish to hire Sally for an alteration; I've a gown that needs adjustment."

"I have no seamstresses available; they've all taken ill," the shop-keeper snarled at Autumn.

Taken aback by the hostility, she snapped a reply, "Why do you lie? I have eyes that work just fine and can clearly see them working in the back. What insult have I ever done to thee, Roger, for you to treat me thus?"

"Lucy has been dead but a fortnight, and already you occupy his lordship's bed. I thought that she was your friend."

Autumn's heart fell as her ire piqued. "Who has spread these falsehoods, for I shall straighten out their tongue quite smartly when I get my hands on them." Roger stepped back from her heated words as she continued in a low growl, "Wish you to know the truth or to continue with the lies? His Grace asked me to make sure that Lucy's belongings were dispensed of properly, and that is what was done. Last night he was summoned by the king and as such hastened to the Rose Palace. He returned just before dawn this morning with the command from our sovereign to marry again by sixth day."

Sally had come up behind Roger as he had spoken with Autumn. "What can I do to help you?" she asked in a hushed tone.

"I am to be married to Lord Edward, and I have a gown that needs altered and adjusted." At her words, a gasp went through the shop and Roger turned white.

He hung his head in shame. "My apologies, milady. We should have known the lies for what they were, as Muriel is known for stirring up trouble with her gossip, yet you have always been gracious and kind."

"Though her tongue be sharp at times," a voice sounded at the entrance to the shop.

Everyone except Autumn bowed as Edward moved in her direction.

"Your Grace, it is an honor."

"Enough," the duke said as he bid them to stand. "I heard the commotion and wished to know the trouble." To Autumn he asked, "Shall I dismiss the girl?"

She shook her head. "No, I shall speak with her and keep her busy, but should it happen again, a punishment for certain."

"You are a generous and forgiving soul," Edward commented as he walked out of the shop, Autumn following. He handed her a purse of coin. "Use this to pay for what is needed." He kissed her cheek and mounted Prince.

Noticing his wet hair, she called after him, "How was the river?"

"Cold!"

Her merry laugh followed him as he left the village.

The week passed quickly as they kept busy with the preparations for the wedding, and soon sixth day was upon them. The heralds proclaimed the arrival of the king and queen, and Autumn grew nervous. She'd not yet changed into her gown, as she was waiting on her sister to assist her in dressing. A commotion in the hall and a knock on the door signaled the arrival of Charilee.

"Enter. It's about time you got here, Charilee; I feared that you had been lost." Autumn turned to her sister only to find Queen Marion standing in front of her. She fell to her knees and lowered her eyes. "Majesty, I am blessed to be in thy presence."

"Stand, dear girl, I wish to see the woman who has finally captured Edward's heart."

Autumn stood as commanded, her eyes remaining downcast. "Look to me, dear," the queen chided, "I wish to judge thy character."

After examining the young woman for several long minutes, the queen waved airily to the gown lying on the bed. "Best be getting dressed. Your groom is waiting."

As she left the room, Autumn grumbled, "Am I a horse to be purchased to be looked upon in such a manner?"

Marion was quite pleased and laughed at Autumn's comment. She'd seen the girl bite her tongue as she'd been looked over. No timid mouse she. The queen was not so obtuse as to not be aware that her cousin-in-law's bride had looked her over as well. Autumn was just not as obvious about it.

Marion was several inches shorter than Autumn, and she judged her to be about as tall as the king. Something Robert would probably find annoying. Her eyes had shown intelligence and curiosity, while her bearing spoke of pride in herself, though not overly so. The queen had sent a handmaiden into the village to inquire about the new duchess-to-be, and the returned information was only positive. She had learned that Autumn, for all her bluster and sharp tongue, was a generous person, poor as she was. She also apparently had a skill for horses and healing, and it was said that her gentle touch was favored over the village healer. Truly a fine mate for Edward, thought the queen as she hurried to the courtyard and her husband's side.

Edward was pacing the small courtyard as his cousin lounged in the chair provided for him. As Marion approached, Robert stood and took her hand. "My dear," he said as he kissed her hand and seated her in the chair beside his and sat again. "What think you of this girl who has so agitated our dear cousin?"

"A fine match, she is equal to the task of taking Edward in hand."

The duke snorted and continued his pacing.

"Cousin, what ails thee? Sit down and be calm," Robert commanded.

"I cannot sit." Edward ran his fingers through his shaggy hair. "What is taking so long? She cares not over much for her appearance. She is trying my patience."

Marion laughed. "Dearest cousin, her sister is wroth with her because she only wished to plait her hair after she had dressed. However, Charilee has held her hostage to be coiffed as fits a duchess. I fear that Autumn is none too pleased at the delay either."

Moments later the heralds sounded the appearance of the bride, and Edward heaved a sigh of relief. A murmur of awe flowed through the guests assembled, and the duke had to blink several times at the vision that stood in front of him. Autumn had chosen his colors for her gown, a deep forest green trimmed at the bodice and hem in silver lace. The long sleeves were slashed to alternate white and green, and her long hair was braided in many rows and wrapped around her head to form a coronet; sprigs of small white flowers and ivy were interwoven into the braids. He stared in wonder at the sight of his bride and started after Robert nudged him in the ribs. "Breathe, cousin," came the whispered command.

Grinning sheepishly, Edward stepped forward and took her arm as her father relinquished the other.

"Who gives this woman away?" the king asked the traditional query.

"I do, Majesty," her father announced in a creaky voice as he bowed before the assembled people.

As he stepped into his place, Autumn murmured to him, "I love you, Papa."

Robert turned his attention to the bride. "Why do you wish to marry this man?"

"Because I love him."

"And will you be loyal and faithful unto him?"

"I will cherish him until my dying day," Autumn stated firmly.

"Will you be obedient to his commands?"

"If they be reasonable requests, Your Majesty, for I am strong-willed and at times apt to see things differently."

Robert stared at her in shock while Edward rolled his eyes, a grin tugging at his lips. Queen Marion snapped open her fan to hide her smile.

"I do vow that I shall never bring him dishonor, milord."

"I can accept that," said the king, finding his voice. He then turned to the groom and asked him similar questions. Soon he proclaimed to the assembled guests, "I give to you the Duke and Duchess of Silver River!" To Edward he said, "Kiss your bride, cousin."

He did so to the cheers of the crowd and led them into the castle for a celebration.

Part 2

Ten years had passed. Autumn and Edward were sound asleep when their nine-year-old twins burst into the room and jumped on the bed. Pouncing on Edward they shouted, "A messenger has come from the king, Father."

Grabbing the boys into a bear hug, he growled, "How dare you wake me from my slumber at this indecent hour."

"Are you going to ignore the king?" both boys queried in unison.

"Nay, I'll not ignore him, you devils. Get out and shut the door behind you."

The twins scurried out of the chamber, slamming the door behind them.

"What could Robert want of you?" Autumn asked as Edward rose and dressed.

"I'll find out soon enough." He bent to kiss her. "Go back to sleep."

As soon as the duke left, she scrambled out of bed and dressed quickly. She plaited her hair into the familiar braid as she hurried down the stairs. As she approached the foyer, she could hear Edward talking quietly with the messenger and the tone put knots in the pit of her stomach.

Spying the duchess, the messenger bowed to her. "Milady, Queen Marion sends greetings to thee."

"'Tis good to see you again, Xander, but I am no fool to think that the queen sends her salutations on a whim so early in the morning. Methinks there is more you came to say." She looked to her husband expectantly.

Edward threw up his hands in agitation. "Might as well hear it from the horse's mouth. You'll only plague me later." To Xander he said, "Come, break your fast at my table."

During the meal, the three sat and talked of little things. When the dishes were cleared from the table and the servants dismissed, Edward indicated that Xander should continue his missive.

"Molsen has usurped the throne of the Realm and has killed all with royal blood. He has set his sights on the Rose Kingdom and has sent raids into our country in an attempt to gain control." Xander paused. "King Robert commands that the Duke of Silver River bring his army to aid in the defense of our country."

Autumn had turned pale at the news as Edward responded, "I shall leave immediately." He stood and called for his man at arms. When the guard appeared, he ordered, "Prepare the men and horses, and gather our weapons and supplies, for the king has need of our aid."

The soldier saluted smartly and went to do his master's bidding; Xander followed him, leaving Edward and Autumn alone.

The duke took his wife into his arms. "My love, 'tis not my wish to leave."

Placing her fingers on his lips, she spoke softly, "Speak no more, for you must do your duty to your king. I am not the only one who risks losing a husband, yet I know that you are strong and shall return to me." Drawing his mouth to hers, she kissed him and said, "I'll get your bag, while you tell the boys of your upcoming adventure."

Edward called for the boys and they came running.

"Father," shouted Arek, "what did the king want of you?"

"Can we come with you?" Charles yelled, not wanting to be outdone by his brother.

The duke took his sons into his arms, as Autumn went to their room to pack his things. Several long minutes later, he joined her. Enclosing her in his embrace from behind, he put his chin upon her head. "I love you, and I swear I'll come home safe and sound."

Turning in his embrace to wrap her arms around him, she muttered into his chest, "See that you do, else the gods of the afterlife will have me to deal with."

"Have you so little faith in me and my ability?"

She looked up at him, her eyes gleaming with unshed tears, and said, "My faith in you is unshakeable, my dearest Edward, but long has it been known of Molsen's treachery and lack of honor. He will stab thee in the back if given half a chance."

Hugging her tight, he told her with conviction, "Then never a chance shall he have. Of course, being the coward that he is, he may not even step onto the battlefield; men of his ilk usually let others do the bloodletting. I vow to you that I shall return a whole and happy man." He kissed her deeply and wiped a stray tear from her cheek as he continued, "I do so love you. Your strength of heart sustains me, and to see your bravery, it gives me the power to overcome my own fear." He picked up the leather bag she had packed and clasped her hand as they made their way to the courtyard. It had been less than half an hour and his men and horses were ready to leave. He handed his bag to a squire to be secured, and his guard handed him his sword. As he belted it on, he looked to his boys and admonished them, "Listen to your mother and take care of her, for you are princes of the kingdom and an example to all."

They bowed to him, expressions solemn, and said in unison, "Will we do as you ask, Father."

He held Autumn tight and kissed her one last time before mounting Prince.

"A moment, my love," she cried as he made to leave, "I must give you and your steed a token." Pulling two ribbons from her braid, she fastened one to Prince's bridle and the other to Edward's sword hilt.

"It shall ever be with me." He kissed her fingers. "I love you." Then he and his men headed down the road to the Rose City to defend their country from a mad man.

Eight months later

Edward sat in his tent, a missive from the king in front of him on the table. He struggled to read the cramped script and wished that Autumn was around to read it to him, as she did at home. She was able to decipher even the most illegible of writing. He sat back in the creaky chair and wearily rubbed the bridge of his nose. It had been nearly a year since he had seen his family, and though his wife wrote to him of the mischief their boys caused and how much they had grown, he missed the chance of being there with them.

He could see in his mind Autumn sitting in the library, the boys at her feet, eyes wide as she spun one of her many tales before bedtime. He thought of her long brown hair as she brushed it out every evening, of her warmth in bed at his side, and of the soft kisses that would awaken him each morning. His heart ached, and he was angry with the madman who had taken him from his hearth and home because of greed. However, the fighting at the border puzzled Edward, as they were merely skirmishes, with little to no blood spilled. If Molsen wanted to conquer the Rose Kingdom, his strategy was very weak.

Several days before, an enemy unit had been discovered in Windy Glen, an interior duchy of the kingdom. No one knew how they had penetrated so deeply into the land as the border was sealed up tight. The battle there had been bloody as Weston had been unprepared, and an entire village had been annihilated, even to the slaughter of the livestock and village animals. It was now nothing more than a smoldering pile of singed earth and stone.

Edward had written Autumn and had asked her to send one of the many copies of the histories to him. He had a feeling that the answer to the puzzle of the foe in Windy Glen could be found within the tome. He put his head in his hands as a sweet memory assaulted him.

A month after their wedding, the duke had found his wife in the library. She had pulled the histories from the shelf and was flipping through the large book; many of the other copies stacked beside her on the mahogany table. Spying Edward, she asked, "Why are there so many hand-copied books of the histories?" He had laughed and told her that as a punishment in his youth he had been made to spend hours copying the very large tome.

She gave him a look. "You must have been a terror to have made so many copies."

He laughed again and pulled her into a hug. "I was the youngest son, so I had plenty of time to get into trouble and mischief. That is until my brothers and mother perished from a fever."

"Milord?" the voice of his squire broke into the duke's thoughts.

"Come in, Richard," he called.

A young man stepped into the tent and executed a slight bow as Edward indicated he should continue.

"The courier has come, sire."

"Send him in."

A few moments after Richard left the tent, a short, dark-skinned man ambled into the tiny space.

"Xander!" exclaimed the duke, happy to see his old friend. "How goes it with you?"

Grinning wearily, the bowlegged man responded, "'Tis been busy, milord. Messages must go around the kingdom day in and day out."

Gesturing for the messenger to sit, Edward said, "What news from Silver River?"

Handing the duke a large square parcel wrapped in cloth, the man sat. "All is well, sire, though you are sorely missed. Young Arek will be quite a warrior someday, and Charles has his mother's gift with horses. But I am certain milady has mentioned such things to you in her letters. She has sent the book you requested as well as a few other items that are still on my saddle."

Edward's heart swelled with pride at hearing such praise of his sons. "Is there anything you need, my friend?"

Xander shook his head. "No, milord. Lady Autumn sees to it that all messengers get food and rest before we leave the castle. Your stable is filled with tired horses, sire, for she sees to it that we have fresh mounts. I fear that her father's farm is depleted of its horses as well, but His Majesty is truly grateful for the assistance. Besides, Silver River horses are the hardiest in the kingdom."

Richard entered the tent with the saddlebags from Xander's horse, deposited them on the cot, and left to resume his other duties. The courier stood and emptied the contents of the bags on the small bed. Edward had moved to Xander's side and watched as he unpacked the bags. There were biscuits and cookies wrapped in a cloth napkin and apples, figs, and dates in one bag. While the other contained drawings and notes in the childish scrawl of his sons, the usual note from Autumn, and a tightly wrapped item in paper. The duke snatched up the strange parcel and found a braided lock of hair and an inscription on the paper.

My love,

    I send this to you so that I can be with you always. You are dearly missed.

Forever yours,
Autumn

He held the tiny plait to his nose, as if to catch a scent of her. He took the letters and drawings to the table to be read later and turned back to the dark-skinned messenger. Picking up an apple, he offered it to Xander, but the man shook his head. "Milady sent a multitude of apples to the camp, sire, and instructed me to take as many as I wanted."

The duke shook his head; it was typical of his wife to be generous. She believed that it set a good example. Before they had wed, she had been a poor farmer's daughter, and though she had no coin or food to offer, she was an excellent healer and would often give her time to assist others or just provide an ear to listen or a shoulder to cry on. Edward was glad that that had not changed.

Apparently, the apple harvest had been very good for her to send so many, and as he followed Xander out of the tent, he stopped and stood agape at the five large wagons that stood in the center of the camp. Autumn had sent more than apples; the wagons were filled with venison, beef, and chicken, potatoes and corn, as well as other foodstuffs. One was filled with warm blankets and clothing, and another was loaded with weapons, horse tack, and metal for horseshoes. It assured Edward that his home was faring well under the rule of his beloved; the supplies were proof that she had rallied the community for the common good.

His squire was instructing some of the men to carry several thick bundles to his tent.

"What is this?" Edward asked as they placed the packages at his feet.

"Items that were to be given to you specifically, under orders from Lady Autumn herself, milord," was Richard's reply.

A cheer was heard from the center of camp as the medicines and bandages were given to the healers.

"Did my wife come as well?" the duke asked in jest.

Xander laughed and said, "She has her hands full in Silver River, sire, but I'm sure if she heard that you needed assistance she'd be here with half of the village in a heartbeat."

Edward laughed in agreement and bid his friend goodbye, instructing him to rest before continuing on his journey, and then he picked up his bundles and carried them into his tent. Opening his packages, he found several tunics made of sturdy cotton, woolen breeches, and two pairs of tough leather boots. Several heavy blankets, long enough to cover him, were accompanied by two very thick pillows. He knew that Autumn had had the clothing and blankets made special for him, because when it came to sewing cloth, she was practically useless, which didn't make sense to him because she repaired harnesses and saddles, and he had even seen her stitch the flesh of their cook one day after she had suffered a deep cut on her hand. The last package was wrapped in silk and very thin, but heavy. Tears filled his eyes as he revealed a sword of the finest quality. He set it gently on his cot and saw that his crest had been etched into the blade and that the hilt was formed of steel oak branches wrapped in forest green leather. The scabbard was fashioned from the finest leather and dyed deep green with thick stripes of silver thread sewn in a serpentine fashion to resemble the river his duchy was named after. A silver ribbon was tied to the hilt with a note attached.

My Dearest Edward,

I had hoped to give this to you when you returned home to us, but it has been a very long year since we have seen you, and I am sure that you have need of it now. The boys and I present this to you with all of our love. I only hope that it shall never have to spill blood. Come home to us soon, for my heart aches with missing you.

Your loving wife and sons

He sat on the edge of his cot, the sword and note held reverently in his hands as he hung his head in sorrow. It had been so long since he had left his family, and he feared that he might never see them again. As the duke sat there, the hair on the back of his neck prickled and he looked up to see a short man in strange black armor standing by the table. The warrior wore a fierce-looking helmet that obscured his features, and before Edward could shout for his guard, the dark knight spoke in a soft voice. "Fear me not, for I come to you in peace. Our peoples are destined to be allies." Gesturing to the cloth-bound bundle on the table, he continued, "Your book will not provide the answers you seek, for it is incomplete."

"Where did you come from?" and though he felt calm the answer chilled his bones.

"I am Darkwater, the warrior that the outlaw in your cousin's palace spoke of so many years ago." The soldier pulled a dagger from his belt and handed it to Edward. "My token of good faith, as what I tell you is true. Molsen will try to conquer your kingdom, but before he can succeed, there are two things he must fulfill."

"He merely stings us and causes no great harm." A thought came to Edward. "Do you know how his men made it to the interior undetected?"

"He has used the magic of the wyvern to enter your country; you must go to Windy Glen. My men will clear your borders."

"The attacks were brutal there, why would Molsen want to destroy the smallest region of the Rose Kingdom?"

"According to prophecy, in that hamlet lives a man who will slay Molsen several years from now. Go now to Weston, your king has commanded it. You are to take control of the army and defeat the interlopers."

"How is it that you know this?"

"It says so in the missive upon your table. The dagger that I have given you will protect you and your men from the wyvern's evil magic and help you determine friend from foe."

Looking at the dagger in his hands, he saw that the hilt was fashioned as a dragon, the mortal enemy of the wyvern. The sheath was metal and fashioned as a dragon facing the one on the hilt; both the hilt and scabbard were inlaid with deep-blue sapphires that seemed to glow with an internal energy all their own.

"How can that be? According to the histories, the wyvern were destroyed centuries ago, and the dragons vanished soon after." The duke looked up from his perusal, but the strangely garbed warrior had vanished as mysteriously as he had appeared.

Edward stood and moved to his table. Lifting the king's missive, he left his tent to order his men to prepare to leave for Windy Glen. It was then that he realized the warrior had not mentioned the second task that Molsen must fulfill to overtake the Rose Kingdom. A soft voice echoed in his head, "Fear not, he will not succeed. The power of the dragon is with you." He looked around, certain that it was the voice of his mysterious visitor, but only saw his men packing up the camp in preparation to move and readying the evening meal.

The heavy sound of pounding hooves indicated a scout returning from the patrol point; he reined his horse in and dismounted in front of the duke. "My lord, the enemy troops are fleeing from our borders."

Edward's head snapped up. "What?"

"They are fleeing as if pursued by demons. Their shrieks of fear filled the air and they ran, leaving everything behind."

"Collect every useful item that you can, but be quick about it. We are ordered to Windy Glen immediately."

The scout saluted and leapt upon his mount to follow his commander's orders.

The strange warrior's words came back to Edward. "My men will clear your borders."

And so they had.

Disorganized chaos reigned as Edward and his men entered Weston's camp. The soldiers of Windy Glen were young men, and

Duke Weston was barely in his twenties, having just inherited his father's title. None in the Rose Kingdom had ever experienced true war, for they had been at peace for centuries. Edward had been an avid student of the histories and the battles that had occurred so long ago, and being an intelligent man, he knew when to employ either a defensive or an offensive strategy during the few fights that had occurred. His men had fared much better than the other forces of the kingdom because of the rigorous training that was required to be in the army of Silver River.

Edward immediately set up his command post and paired his men with those of Windy Glen. One man caught his eye and he asked, "Weston, do you know that young man, the tall one speaking with Xander?"

"He is Dalon, an orphan raised by the blacksmith and his wife."

"How did his parents die?"

"No one knows, sire. He was found as an infant in a field after the spring rains twenty years ago."

Darkwater's words came back to Edward: "In that hamlet lives a man who will slay Molsen, and he will be a strong force in the alliance between my country and yours."

He shook his head to clear it and instructed the younger man, "Send him to me."

"At once, milord."

The duke was writing a letter to Autumn when Dalon was escorted to his tent by Weston.

The young soldier bowed respectfully and said, "I'm honored, Lord Edward, to be called to your service. How may I serve?"

Edward looked the man over and asked, "The sword on your hip, how skilled are you with it?"

"As well as can be expected for one new to the weapon, sire. I'm more familiar with the tools of a blacksmith or a farrier than a soldier."

"I will place you under Fallon's guidance and he will teach you the basic stances of swordplay."

"As you command, milord."

*****

It was quiet for the moment, save for the moans and cries of the injured. It was a brief respite from the fighting as both sides collected their wounded and regrouped. A disturbance at the edge of the camp caught Edward's attention and he prepared to do battle. Three of the largest warhorses he had ever seen made their way slowly to his tent, and he relaxed slightly as he recognized the middle knight as the man who had visited him several weeks earlier. The two men on either side were large and tall much like their mounts. The duke's men stood away from the strangely clad warriors, warily eyeing the wicked weapons that hung from the saddles.

"Your borders have been cleared, Lord Edward. Now I shall remove Molsen's ability to move his men into your lands and foil his bloodthirsty quest for another throne. It will be up to you to dispatch the remainder of the army trapped here, but I assure you that no more reinforcements will follow."

The red-haired giant to Darkwater's left handed him a long iron rod with a pointed spike on one end, the other had a fist sized oval gem that was crystal clear. Edward found it odd that the men had removed their helmets when their commander had not. The warrior seemed even smaller than he remembered, but the duke passed it off as an illusion because of the mammoth horses. Darkwater dismounted and spun the spike with a flourish before slamming it into the ground with such force that the Rose Kingdom soldiers were in awe of the slender man's strength. Only the gem remained above the ground. The warrior then began to speak with force in a language that the duke knew for certain was ancient and long dead.

"Let the portal close and shut out the foe, and by the strength of my people let it remain closed forevermore." The dark warrior swung his broadsword and struck the gem embedded in the earth; it shattered to dust and no sign that the gem or the rod had ever existed remained.

A shiver of fear ran down Edward's spine at the power this man commanded.

Darkwater remounted and said to the duke, "It is done. You shall be victorious."

53

He turned his steed, and his men followed as they made their way out of the camp, but stopped as a wounded soldier collapsed in front of them. Edward's men were quick to pick the man up, and the duke saw that it was Dalon who had been injured. The dark knight dismounted and commanded the men to hold fast. Taking Dalon's head into his hands, he again spoke the strange language. Miraculously the wounds began to fade and the soldier's strength returned. As the three men stood looking at Darkwater with awe and fear, he spoke to Dalon in a voice that carried through the camp with power.

"Fight bravely, for your truth shall be known and all will fear, first for you, then with you. But fear the enemy naught, for you shall live long and well." The strange warrior mounted his steed and nudged it into motion, and the three knights vanished into the dark forest surrounding the camp.

"Do you know who they were, sire? Where do they hail from?" Weston asked Edward.

Answering carefully, the duke responded as he returned to his tent, "Your guess is as good as mine. However, I believe that there will be no more reinforcements from Molsen. Come, let us see how we can purge the rest of his vermin from our land."

The final battle was fierce and bloody, but Darkwater's words spoke true: no fresh recruits arrived to strengthen the enemy lines to harry the exhausted troops of the Rose Kingdom. The men were heartened, and victory was assured once the foe realized that their forces were not being replenished. Edward made it a habit to ride through each of the soldiers' camps encouraging the men. Although most of the fighting was done, minor skirmishes would break out and men were still defending their land.

The duke came across such a fight as he reached his own camp. Several dozen enemy soldiers had ambushed his men when they returned from the field with the wounded. He could see that even the wounded were battling the foe where able, swinging swords or shooting arrows into the mass of men. Edward kicked his horse to a canter and entered the fray sweeping away pikes with his sword; an arrow pierced his left shoulder, but he ignored the pain and focused on defeating the enemy. The attacking soldiers were soon subdued and order to the camp restored, but as the duke turned his horse to his tent, his squire shouted a warning, and as he looked up, a mace struck the left side of his helmet. He thrust his sword into the villain's heart as the horse ran by then collapsed over Prince's shoulder; he saw his enemy fall dead from his mount through a curtain of blood as everything went dark. His last thought was of the promise he had made to Autumn about coming home whole and hardy.

The months came and went, and news of the battles came often to Autumn. Every week the duke sent a letter describing his adventures and professing his love for his family. Every second day, the duchess would wait in the courtyard for the courier's arrival, a missive of her own to send back to her beloved. This day, however, no rider came, though Autumn did not worry, for it had happened that the messenger would arrive the next day. Yet when no news had arrived by sixth day, she was filled with dread.

Calling Arek and Charles to her, she said, "Pack some clothes and go to Grandfather's. Take old Apollo and Othello, for the green grasses of his pastures shall soothe their spirits. I wish for you to stay there until I call for you."

"Has something happened to Father?" queried a subdued Arek.

Hugging them to her, she said, "I've not received any word this week, so I must go to the palace. I wish you to go to the farm as your grandparents may need your help."

"We will do as you ask, Mother," Charles said softly.

After seeing the boys off with their nanny and two servants, she ordered her horse to be readied. To the head housekeeper she said, "Please see that our rooms are cleaned, and should you need aid of any kind, seek it from my father. But I feel that all shall remain safe here in Silver River."

"Our prayers go with thee, milady. I do so hope the duke is well."

"Can you bring me several pots of the salve? I feel that I must help somehow, and healing I know well."

As the maid returned and handed the requested items to be placed on the pack horse, a horseman galloped up the drive. His clothing hung in rags about him, and he seemed as if he were about to fall from his mount in fatigue. The poor creature was lathered and hung its head in exhaustion as the messenger brought the horse to a halt.

"Milady," his voice was barely a whisper, "a message from the king. The fighting is over and we have been victorious over the madman of the Realm. But your husband has been badly wounded and your presence is commanded in the royal city."

"Get down from your horse and take rest inside," Autumn commanded the man.

"My orders are to escort you to the palace, milady."

"Nonsense, I know the way and am quite capable of making the journey with my men. Your horse can barely stand and you are all but falling off his back. Sleep, bathe, and eat, then follow when you are better rested."

After seeing that the king's herald was taken care of, Autumn mounted her gelding and headed to the royal city at a gallop. Her heart afraid of what might be waiting for her there.

The journey seemed to take forever, though only an hour had gone by. She was loathe to push the horses too hard, but worry for Edward kept her to a fast pace. She heaved a sigh of relief as the city came into view. Soon she was at the castle gates. Racing into the courtyard, she dismounted and let the reins dangle as she rushed into the palace.

"Where is Lord Edward's chamber?" she demanded of a passing servant. She hurried to the suite of rooms that had been indicated and pushed open the doors with a bang. The odor that accosted her made her gag, and seeing the state of the room angered her. "Is the healer trying to kill this man?" she shouted.

Several servants had come at her bellow and she snapped at them, "Get the windows open and the fire banked, for he shall surely die from the heat."

Going to the bed, she called for a lantern to be brought and threw open the curtains. The sight she beheld brought a bellow of rage to her throat. "Get me that fool healer this instant!"

Tearing open all of the bed curtains and tying them at the posts, she beheld the pale form of her beloved. Two long ragged wounds covered the left side of his face and had been left to fester. Drawing the blanket back slowly, she wept at what she found: an arrow wound in his left shoulder, a deep cut on his right thigh, and a myriad of other little nicks and bruises about his entire body. All were infected, and she wondered at the ability of the healer to remain employed.

"What are you doing?" an indignant little man demanded. "He'll catch his death of cold."

Autumn straightened to her full height, a trick learned from Edward, and turned the whole of her fury on the healer. "You incompetent fool. He may die because of the infection that has set in. Did it not occur to you that the wounds should be cleaned and stitched?" He backed away from her, but she followed, her voice little more than a hiss. "Get thee gone from my sight and pray that Edward recovers, for I vow that my dagger shall pierce your heart should he die."

The man turned and scurried from the room in fear, as Autumn commanded the servants to bring her the items needed to heal her husband. "I need buckets of hot and cold water, a clean sharp knife, and a multitude of clean bandages." She looked up to see the men and women standing mutely and she lost her temper. "Are you deaf? Do as I have commanded!" As one they moved to do her bidding. She called for ale and opiates. "I shall need a stout stick as well, be sure it is clean. Bring me silk thread and a curved needle." The items were brought to her, and as the room cooled, she set about to heal her husband properly.

Calling to a page, she handed him a coin. "Go to the apothecary and purchase witch hazel, then bring the jars of salve from my saddle. Do it in a thrice and I'll give you two coin."

Autumn set the knife in the fire to heat, and after several minutes, she pulled it out, rinsed it in a bucket of hot water, and wiped it carefully with a clean cloth. "I shall need four stout men to hold him down."

"I can help," proclaimed the king. "My cousin is dear to me."

"Place this stick between his teeth, milord, and hold him tightly, but have a care with his injured shoulder. I shall start with the wounds on his face."

When all was ready, the duchess took a deep breath, climbed upon the bed, and whispered into her husband's ear, "My love, this shall hurt, but 'tis necessary to save your life."

With a steady hand, she drew the knife down the angry red lines on his face, the pus oozing from the cuts. Wiping the infection with clean cloths, she pressed gently on the wounds to be sure that they were clear. "Hold him tight," she instructed the men as she prepared the witch hazel, "for this shall sting and he may thrash." After rinsing his face with clean water, she threaded the curved needle with the silk thread and slowly stitched each gash closed.

"He'll have an awful scar, milady," said Robert from the side of the bed where he held tight to his cousin's arm.

"I think not, Majesty, as my stitches are small, and when healed, naught but very thin lines will be seen, and only up close."

"You are that confident in your skill?"

"I am, milord."

After she had finished stitching his face, Autumn slathered the wounds with the salve and left them open to the air. She turned her attention to the shoulder wound and asked that Edward be lifted so that she could see the extent of the injury.

"'Tis good that the arrow missed the bone. The muscle has been torn, but with rest it should heal, if the infection has not done more damage." Again, she cleansed and closed the wound muttering about the incompetence of the king's healer. Moving from the more serious wounds to the minor, she checked the duke from head to toe, making sure that no injury went unnoticed. Satisfied that all was fine, she bathed him gently with soft cloths and warm water.

She instructed the servants to change the sheets, and when Edward was ensconced in his bed once more, Autumn said to the king, "I am worried, for he has not made a move nor a sound, and even in a fever sleep, the pain should have affected him somewhat." Laying her ear upon the duke's chest, she continued, "His heart beats strong, but I have seen the body live even after the mind has died.

Your healer had better pray that my husband lives, else he shall feel my wrath unleashed."

Robert embraced his cousin's wife as she straightened and assured her, "Fear not for his life. Already the pallor that was upon him is fading, and always he has had a great stamina for pain. You must be tired, but before you rest, I have a boon to ask of thee."

"If I can fulfill it, Majesty, I shall."

"Please, there is no need to be formal. Call me Robert. Marion is ill, and I wish for you to see to her. She falls ill at times, and this new healer brushes off our concerns saying that it is naught but the vapors."

Autumn snorted with derision. "Thy healer is a sham, and he should be lashed for his fakery. Take me to the queen, sire, and I shall help her if I can."

After placing a cool cloth on Edward's forehead, she followed Robert to the queen's chambers. The room was dark and stifling hot when they entered, and she instructed the servants to dampen the fire and open the shutters.

"Light bothers Her Majesty, milady," said a servant girl as Autumn moved to open the bed curtains.

"Then I'll leave this curtain closed." Turning to the king, she asked, "What are her symptoms?"

Sitting wearily into a chair near the bed, he responded, "She becomes sensitive to light and sound, a fierce ache pounds her brow and upsets her stomach."

"Vapors, my arse," snorted Autumn, startling Robert with her expletive. "Queen Marion suffers from migraines, milord, which are quite easy to treat. Most times they can even be prevented."

"Indeed?"

"Aye, have you any java?"

"I don't know what it is."

"'Tis a strong drink made from the ground beans of a plant. It has a substance within that helps reduce the pain of certain head-aches. A cool bath and having her drink plenty of water will also help. Keep her chambers cool and dimly lit; use only covered lanterns as the flickering of candles can exacerbate the headaches. I don't suggest the use of opiates unless the pain is severe."

"Truly, you have set my fears to rest." Robert stood and embraced Autumn. "Where can I find these java beans?"

"If you have a rider, my father's farm grows them. He also has bags that have been roasted and freshly ground."

"I shall send a man immediately. Now get yourself bathed and to bed, cousin, for tomorrow will be a better day."

Autumn hurried back to Edward's chambers. After dismissing the servants, she bathed quickly and crawled into bed at his side. He was still warm from the fever, but satisfied that it had lessened, she fell fast asleep.

*****

Edward opened his eyes to the morning light. He felt stiff and sore, and he wondered at the ache in his face. He moved to sit and moaned as pain shot through his left shoulder. He saw that it was swathed in bandages; he also spied a cloud of brown hair on the pillow beside him. Using his good arm, he lifted the blanket and discovered his beloved fast asleep. Lying back, he covered her and laughed softly to himself. She'd come to him and had probably set the royal household on its ear.

"You mustn't move too much or you could tear your stitches," came Autumn's muffled voice. "I did not spend so many hours closing your wounds to have you open them again." She sat up and placed a hand in the center of his chest. Her brown eyes checked him over quickly. "How do you feel, milord?" She peered into his eyes.

"Poorly, for you have forgotten my name," he teased, his blue-gray eyes twinkling with mirth.

Taking care not to jostle his injuries, she straddled his stomach, causing him to grunt. "Jest not with me for you hung between life and death, and had you died, the fool healer would have followed."

"Then lucky for him that I live," he said. Using his good arm, he tugged at her hair. "Give me a kiss, for long has it been since I saw you last."

Autumn smiled. "A gentle one today, my dear, for thy face must heal as well. A wicked weapon it was to leave such a mark on you."

"A mace struck my helmet, and the metal broke and cut me. I shall have scars that maim my face for thee."

"Oh, foolish man, no visible scar shall remain. My stitches are neat and small. Methinks your looks shall have improved."

"I wish to see my cousin—"

Autumn cut him off with a kiss. "That cannot be, my dear, for you have no strength within you. You have been asleep for fifteen days." She moved off Edward and checked his shoulder and leg wounds, leaving his face for last.

"How can that be?"

"When the mace struck you, it knocked you unconscious. Your squire found you sprawled upon Prince's back, blood flowing freely from your head. He brought you back here where that charlatan of a healer allowed your wounds to fester and left you to languish in a fever for nearly a week. I had received no word from you and was ready to set out for the palace when Robert sent a man to get me." Autumn paused and brushed Edward's hair back from his face. Caressing his uninjured cheek, she continued, "When I first came in, it smelled of death, and I feared you had been lost. I became a demon and ordered everyone about, even Robert. When I saw your face, I despaired, for the wound was angry and infected. I worried that you did not flinch and feared that the fool healer had overdosed you with the opiates, but your heart was beating strong. I concluded that whatever caused your facial injury could have jarred your brain."

"I know that you have skill at healing, but to stitch the flesh of your beloved could not have been an easy thing for you." Edward twirled a strand of her long brown hair betwixt his fingers, tugging her closer to his face. "Kiss me again, for thy love will give me strength."

"You've had naught to eat, save for the broth that I poured down your throat. You are but a shadow of the man you were. Take it slow, my love, else you fall ill again." She kissed him, and thus the king found them.

"I say, cousin, you gave us quite a scare. Your wife brought you back from the edge of death; methinks with sheer will. I dare say that the healer will be happy to hear that you live, although not so much with his situation."

Startled by Robert's booming voice, the lovers pulled apart. Autumn helped Edward to sit and supported him with pillows. She then excused herself to get dressed.

"A magnificent woman," said the king. "She loves you dearly, cousin. When she found you in such a horrid state, she threatened the healer that if you died, her dagger would pierce his heart. Not many men can claim a love as strong as that."

Adjusting himself against his pillows, wincing as he jostled his arm, Edward said, "I thank the gods for her every day. Have you any food? I am famished."

Robert laughed. "Nay, be assured that your wife will take care of that, but beware, because the fare may not be what you're used to."

"What do you mean?"

"In the short time that she has been here, she has aided many of the other soldiers. Autumn can be quite the bully when healing is her concern."

"'Tis a trait that she learned on her father's farm."

"She also nursed some of the injured horses; she does have a knack for those animals. Prince is doing well in the stable, and Richard is a fine squire. He brought you home to us."

A commotion at the door attracted the men's attention. Autumn was directing the servants to place several steaming trays of food upon a table. As she shooed them from the room, Queen Marion entered and took a place at the table.

"Come, Robert, eat with me here," she said.

As the king moved to the queen's side, he shot a grin at his cousin.

Autumn had grabbed a bowl and sat on the edge of the bed at Edward's side. His gray-blue eyes flashed in annoyance. "I can feed myself, woman!"

"Hardly," she spat back. "You could barely keep your eyes open whilst speaking with your cousin. So still thy tongue and open your mouth."

Edward obediently ate the porridge his wife spooned up for him, as he did feel his strength waning, and he was grateful for her assistance.

"Do not fear, Edward," Marion called from the table, "you'll be hale and hearty in no time at all."

However, he did not hear, for after the last spoonful, he had fallen asleep. Autumn smoothed his hair and kissed his forehead. "Sleep well, my love." She adjusted his pillows and blankets, pausing momentarily to trail her fingers across his chest, still muscular even after all he'd been through. She checked his bandages again, and satisfied that everything was fine, she joined her cousins at the table.

"I have not thanked you yet for helping me with my headaches, but the java is a bitter drink to swallow," said the queen.

"I am glad that it was a simple thing. If you drink the java, hot, with sweetener and cream, it should make it finer for thy palate."

"So is my cousin going to be fine? Or are there other ailments to expect?" the king queried.

Autumn thought a moment before answering. "I think that he shall be fine as he is strong, but I wish to use caution, for I've seen injuries such as his take down a healthy man as an ax fells a tree. His eyes are clear and his memory seems sound, but I still think that he should go slowly."

"He can be a bear when forced to sit idle. Can you handle his temperament?"

"Before I married Edward, sire, I was a fine hand at breaking in saddle horses on my father's farm. All that is needed is a firm hand and patience."

A week later Autumn's patience had worn thin. Edward was a stubborn man, and it was all she could do to keep him in bed.

"Hold still, fool," she growled at him as she tried to inspect the wound on his face. "It's time to remove the stitches."

"I wish to get up. I've had enough of lying about in bed," he yelled back at her.

Placing a hand in the center of his chest, she pushed him back into his pillows. "When I can no longer easily push you back, then you may get out of bed and walk about. You are still weak, but after I remove the stitches, you can try to stand a bit."

He agreed and sat still as stone while Autumn slowly and painstakingly removed the silken threads from his cheek. Once finished, she smoothed salve over the tiny scars. She sighed. "You are still a handsome devil."

He grimaced at her delay and demanded, "My shoulder wants your attention."

"Truly you are a grouch and an ungrateful wretch to treat me so foully," she said, moving to his shoulder, tears filling her eyes. He remained silent as she removed the stitches from his remaining wounds and wrapped them tightly in clean bandages.

Grabbing her hand as she turned to leave, he apologized, "I am a fool to be so grumpy. You have done everything for me and I haven't made it easy." He pulled her close and wiped a stray tear from her cheek. "Your strength is such that at times I forget that your heart is tender. I beg your forgiveness."

Brushing the hair from his forehead, she smiled sadly. "I do so love you, and because of the injury to your head, I wish you to be careful of pushing too hard. A relapse could kill you." She bent and kissed him softly. "You are forgiven."

He grasped her braid before she could move away and tugged her close. "I beg from you another kiss, and it is lonely in this bed when you are gone."

She complied, and though he was still weak, he pulled her onto the bed and sealed his mouth to hers in a searing kiss.

Lying breathless beside side him, Autumn whispered, "How I miss your gentle touch, yet you are not yet strong enough." She ran her fingers down the length of his chest. "Do you wish to try and stand?"

His heated eyes met hers and he managed a nod. She helped him to sit and swing his legs over the side of the bed. Using the bedpost and Autumn's shoulder as support, he stood, but only for a few moments. He sat heavily on the bed and grumbled, "I cannot even stand. When will this weakness pass?"

"Lay upon your stomach," Autumn ordered and kissed his good cheek. "I have something that may help you, but remember you must go slowly."

Edward did as she asked and groaned as her small but strong hands kneaded his unused muscles. He sighed in pleasure as she moved from his arms to his back. Sitting astride him, she massaged the tight cords at the back of his legs and buttocks. When his soft snores permeated the quiet of the room, Autumn slipped off and covered him with a light blanket. Stroking his broad back once more, she placed a kiss on his head and left the room.

"Enough with your nagging, woman," the duke shouted, "I can feed myself!"

Autumn had had more than her share of attitude from her husband, and taking the bowl from his hands, she dumped it over his head. "Fine. Feed yourself, bathe yourself, and dress yourself, for I'll not be doing it again!" Leaving the bowl upon his head, she stormed out of the room, slamming the door behind her.

Edward looked to his cousin in disbelief, porridge running down his face. The king tried to stifle a laugh, but it burst through against his will.

"It's not funny, Robert," the duke growled. "It's a sticky mess."

"'Tis your own fault, cousin," laughed Robert. "Methinks you aggravate her on purpose."

"Why would I do such a thing?"

"Because you have nothing else to do and are bored by your confinement here. She makes a fetching sight with her eyes aglitter and cheeks flushed."

Edward smiled ruefully. "That she does." He removed the bowl from his head, scooted to the edge of the bed, and said, "Cousin, assist me to the bath chamber, I wish to wash this porridge off."

"I'll help you, but only if you take it slow. Your wife would have my hide should harm befall you here and now."

Robert supported his cousin on the short walk to the bath, and once the duke was settled in the warm water, the king sent servants in to change the bedding and clean the room. Edward leaned back in the large tiled tub, weary from the short jaunt to the bath. He lounged for several long minutes before gathering the cake of soap and attempting to lather his body. He examined his wounds closely, and though they were tender to the touch, they had healed well. Only very thin scars remained, and he marveled at the skill with which his wife had stitched him up. He felt guilty and angry with himself for his outburst. He leaned his head against the side of the tub and closed his eyes, struggling not to weep at the hurt he knew he had caused her.

"Lean forward, Edward," Autumn's voice whispered in his ear, "I need to scrub your back."

Opening his eyes, he beheld her face, her eyes slightly swollen from tears, and he realized that she was in the bath with him.

"Milady," he said in a choked voice, "no man is more blessed than I to have a mate like thee."

Plucking a clump of porridge from his hair, she smiled softly. "I should have been more patient with you. I know how much your heart despises your imposed idleness, and for that I am sorry." Pushing him to turn, she said, "Now, let me bathe you proper."

Autumn took a soft cloth and lathered it with the soap; she ran it over his broad shoulders, back, and chest, which were still fairly muscled though he'd been abed nearly a month. She trailed the cloth over and under his arms, paying close attention to his sore shoulder. Rinsing the cloth, she gently wiped his face, taking care of his injured cheek. Bidding him to dunk his head, she lathered his hair and kneaded his scalp with her fingertips. She had him dunk again to rinse away the suds. She moved and took first one foot then the other as she worked her way up and massaged each leg, being cautious of his newly healed wounds. She let the cloth slide over his hips and buttocks. Moving to his belly, she continued lower until she reached his groin. He grabbed her then in a fierce embrace and kissed her hard.

"Thou art a saucy wench to tease me so, knowing how weak I am," he growled huskily after moving his mouth from hers.

She lay atop of him, her loose hair covering his chest and shoulders. Her eyes were glazed with passion and she struggled for composure as she replied, "You have regained some strength, milord."

He set her in front of him and returned her ministrations. He was soon fatigued, however, and said, "Perhaps I should get back to bed."

Autumn helped him back to the bedchamber and dried him with a thick, soft towel much the way she had washed him. He then lay on the freshly made bed, and as she crawled in beside him and pulled the blankets up, they fell asleep in each other's arms.

When Edward woke, it was nearing suppertime, and a smiling Autumn greeted him. Holding out his breeches and tunic, she announced, "'Tis time for you to get up and walk a bit."

With her help he dressed quickly and donned his boots. She handed him a thick walking stick that he used as support from the bed to the door. Still holding his stick, he held her hand as they made their way slowly to the royal dining room. As soon as the duke entered, a cheer erupted from the assembled men at the many tables. Two young men came forward and Edward's eyes filled with tears. His two sons, whom he'd not seen in nearly a year, had grown, and he could see the men they would soon become. They embraced their father and assisted him to his seat at the head table beside the king as Autumn followed. After their mother was seated next to the duke, the boys returned to the table where Edward's men at arms sat.

King Robert stood and the room quieted. Raising his goblet, he proclaimed, "To Lord Edward, whose skill in battle and knowledge of strategy helped save our kingdom."

The soldiers stood and stomped their feet upon the floor as the gathered nobles beat their fists upon the tables in honor of the royal duke.

The king signaled for silence, and as it fell, he raised his cup again. "To Lady Autumn, his wife, who has returned our cousin to the living." At this, Robert turned and bowed low to Autumn. The nobles stood and followed his example as the ranks of fighting men went to their knees in honor of the duchess, for many had also felt her gentle touch of healing.

Edward took her hand and lifted it to his lips. "Your strength has made me whole again, and for this I honor you, milady."

When the commotion settled down and the feast was underway, Robert leaned around his cousin and said to Autumn, "I'll grant you anything you ask of me, for much do I owe thee for Edward's life and Marion's relief."

"Sire, I need nothing. I have a home, a loving husband, and a family; I truly need no more than that. But I would ask that a school be set up to train those with a healing talent properly."

"A splendid idea, but what do I do with him?" Robert indicated the former healer standing between two of the royal guard.

"Pardon him and apprentice him where his talents lay, milord."

"Truly, you are a forgiving soul," the king said as he motioned for the guard to bring the man to him.

The room grew quiet as Robert stood and spoke to the prisoner, "Lady Autumn has asked that you be pardoned, but you shall never practice healing again. You will be sent to the scholars and they will determine what useful skills and talents that you have. Do not disappoint, for the punishment was to have been execution for the falsification of your position."

The former healer fell to his knees and prostrated himself before the duchess. "I thank you, milady, for your forgiveness, granting me mercy, and speaking on my behalf to the king. I vow that I shall find my true calling and follow it with my whole being." He stood and the guard escorted him to his new quarters.

*****

"The party went on long into the night, and happy was the royal household, for the kingdom had been saved. A fortnight later, the duke was fully recovered and, bidding his cousins goodbye, took his family home."

The woman's husband leaned over her chair and kissed her cheek. "That's my favorite story."

The children were wide-eyed with wonder at the tale, and the youngest piped up, "But, Grandfather, Grandmother has never told that story before."

Leaning down and lifting the boy into his strong arms, the grandfather replied with a mischievous smile, "I know."

The two men looked to their father and spoke in unison, "Did Mother truly call you a fool in front of the whole village?"

The woman laughed as he nodded, a grin on his face.

The oldest girl's eyes lit up. "The story was about you and Grandfather, wasn't it? He is the duke." Peering at her grandfather's face, she said, "But I see no scars."

"And you won't," said he, "for your grandmother's healing skill is unsurpassed."

"Grandmother, did our cousin Matek ever form the alliance with Darkwater?" the oldest boy asked.

"Is Darkwater Forest as scary as everyone says?" asked the youngest from the safety of his grandfather's arms.

Autumn and Edward exchanged glances then looked to their sons before Autumn answered, addressing all of her grandchildren, "That is a story for another day."

Arek stood and took his son from Edward's arms and passed him to his wife. "Say good night, children. It is well past your bedtime."

The children obeyed, although the older ones grumbled and followed their mothers out of the massive library. Arek and Charles embraced their parents as Charles said with awe in his voice, "What an honorable responsibility we have to preserve and protect the secrets of Darkwater."

Arek nodded his agreement as they said good night and left for their respective rooms. Edward took Autumn's hand, and when she was standing, they looked to the mantle of the great fireplace where the dragon dagger was proudly displayed, the sapphires glowing softly in the dying firelight.

"I'm surprised the children did not see it. They'd have had you telling them about dragons for certain," Edward said with a soft chuckle.

Autumn merely smiled as she led him to their warm bed.

A small figure in fierce armor stepped from the shadows as the duke and his wife left the chamber. He placed a matching dagger encrusted with emeralds next to the other on the mantle.

"Sleep well, my friends, for a terrible war is on the horizon, and I shall need your help." He disappeared back into the shadows, and all was peaceful and still.

About the Author

Jo Estell was born in Rochester, New York, in 1973. In 1978, her family moved to Pinellas Park, Florida. She now lives in St. Petersburg, Florida, with her husband and five cats. She is an avid fan of fantasy and science fiction. Jo is a serious animal lover and has grown up with a myriad of pets throughout her life with special affection for cats and squirrels. Her favorite theme park is Animal Kingdom at the Walt Disney World Resort.